The Most Beautiful Bully

Shannon Freeman

SADDLEBACK
EDUCATIONAL PUBLISHING

S

The Most Beautiful Bully

Silentious

The Alternative

All About My Selfie

www.sdlback.com

ISBN-13: 978-1-68021-006-4
ISBN-10: 1-68021-006-8
eBook: 978-1-63078-288-7

Printed in Guangzhou, China
NOR/0215/CA21500035

19 18 17 16 15   1 2 3 4 5

Acknowledgements

First, I have to thank God. This has been a dream come true. I've picked up books and read the authors' biographies all my life, wondering how they did what they did. I never thought that one day I would be an author myself. It was beyond my imagination at the time. But God said "Yes!" and here I am today.

I would like to thank Saddleback Educational Publishing for entrusting me with this new venture. I was headed in the direction of another high school series when Arianne approached me about focusing my writing on middle school students. This series has blessed my life so much. I am happy to write books that my nieces and nephews can read. What a blessing!

Thank you to my readers. I try hard to write books that you can relate to so that you can find a piece of yourselves in the characters. I hope that I have hit the mark.

Thank you, Felise Collins. You keep me accurate. You are my little middle-school insider and keep me abreast about this emerging generation. Love you!

Thank you, Mama! I would not be able to do any of this if you weren't there to pick up the pieces. Thank you for helping me, believing in me, and loving me unconditionally.

Thank you to my kiddos. You are my reason. I push, fight, scrap, and get the job done because of you. I just want you to be proud of your mom. Love my babies.

And the last shall be first … thank you to my husband, who is always by my side. I love you more than words can say. God gave me the best he had to offer. The sky is the limit. I love you.

Dedication

To those out there who are living or have lived this story. Just know, this too shall pass. Keep your head held high, get help, and know that it's more the bully's problem than your problem. You are beautifully and wonderfully made.

Chapter 1

The First of Many

It was a cool fall day in Texsun City on the Texas Gulf Coast. Carson Roberts shivered as she ran from the warmth of home to the cold of her mom's beat-up old Honda Accord. A car that had been around for as long as she could remember.

Carson was starting a new school today: Summit Middle School.

"It's a great opportunity," her mother said. "You will love it."

"It's really an honor," her mother said.

"You're too smart for your other school," her mother said.

Her mother said many things. Everything except what Carson was supposed to do after transferring midstream.

She had to leave behind all of her friends to go to Summit. The school was across town and catered to Texsun City's brightest students. They were the ones who "showed great promise" as others in the community liked to say.

This was the first year that Summit would bus students in from urban schools, allowing disadvantaged kids to benefit from a program that had been designed for the community's elite. Carson would soon ride the bus too. But her mother opted to drive her there for the first few days.

The school was located near the coast. That's where the town's wealthiest lived.

Anyone else interested in a superior education had to apply, then be accepted. The school looked at everything: state exams, grades, and personality.

Mothers could be heard in grocery stores, bragging that their child had been accepted. Carson's name was not on the original list of students admitted. She was waitlisted. But her mother didn't stop until her daughter was in: one of Summit's fifty new sixth, seventh, and eighth graders.

"You're in, Carson! A seventh-grade spot opened up. Someone dropped out. Better a few weeks late than never," she said as she held her daughter's acceptance letter in her hand.

Carson knew that her mother had worked hard to get her in. But it didn't make it any easier. "I'm going to miss my friends," she complained. She knew that her mother would never understand.

"Jody will be right here when you get

home. She lives across the street. You hit a wall at Carver Middle School. Mama wants more for you."

Carson rolled her eyes. She knew that her mother was right. But it didn't make it any easier.

As their car turned a corner, she could see the sign:

Summit Middle School
Striving for Excellence

It grew bigger and bigger as they approached her new school. It wasn't like Carver at all. It was a newly built school, home to around three hundred middle school students. Summit had a reputation. The kids were privileged and snobby. That's all Carson knew and all she wanted to know.

"I don't want to get out," she protested, watching groups of students laugh and joke as they entered the school. Friendships had already been made. Cliques had already formed.

Her mom let out a big sigh and turned to her. Grabbing her daughter's hands, she gently kissed them both. "I love you, baby. Does Mama ever guide you down the wrong path?"

Carson shook her head as her eyes studied the cracked leather of the passenger seat.

"Exactly. Now look at me. This is a good thing for you. There's a price to pay for what you want in life."

"I don't want to go to school with preppy rich kids, Mom. I was fine at Carver Middle. Just let me go back."

"No, I can't … *we* can't do that. Move forward. You'll be fine."

Carson looked out the window as the sea of middle schoolers filed into the redbrick building. No graffiti had ever covered these walls. She was sure it never would. She knew her mother was right. But it wouldn't be like her if she didn't first put up a fight.

Carson got out of the car, clutching her new schedule tightly, as if it were her mother's hand. She walked down the long path toward the doors. When she entered the building, it was like entering a foreign world. There was so much school pride displayed in the front hall you would think these people bled black and gold. It was very Disney Channel. She was light years away from Carver, and she knew it.

Just as she rounded the corner, she ran smack dab into someone—a very annoyed someone.

"Ew! Watch where you are going!" screamed a girl who would have been pretty if her face didn't look as though she had swallowed two-day-old sushi.

"I'm so sorry. I'm just—"

"You're just what? Who even cares?"

She tossed her blonde ponytail, smacking Carson in the face with its strawberry-shampoo scent. And *that* was the first person Carson encountered at Summit. She took a slow, deep breath.

Just like I thought, total snots, she thought as she continued on her quest to locate her first class.

"Excuse me," she said to a man with a bullhorn. He was telling everyone to keep moving and get to first period.

"Get to class!" he yelled, making her wince at the loudness of his voice as it vibrated through the bullhorn.

"But … but …" Carson stammered.

He looked at her as if she had fallen off the stupid truck. Carson thrust her schedule into his hands. She was unable to get her thoughts together. So much was happening at once. "Where do I go?" she finally said.

"Is this your first day?" he asked,

confused. He looked down at her schedule. It wasn't often that students started later in the school year. "I'm Vice Principal Briggs. Come with me. I'll show you to your first class," he said, changing his tone.

She had not been far away. She was still a bit jittery as she entered the classroom. Carson didn't look at the other students' faces as Mr. Briggs introduced her to the teacher.

"This is Carson Roberts," he said to the white-haired English teacher already working diligently with groups of students. She welcomed Carson and assigned her to the smallest group.

"You need to get Carson caught up on what's going on. Make her feel welcomed." The teacher nodded at the group of students and smiled.

Carson looked at the kids in her group. They were diverse, to say the least. Something she wasn't used to at her other school. There were only five white students at Carver. But this group consisted of three white kids, one Asian girl, and her. What was cool was that everyone was working together to make the project a success. At Carver she would have been the only one working. Carson would have been up all night trying to pull it off.

She took her seat. The kids explained the plot of *Where the Red Fern Grows*. They caught her up on their project.

When the bell rang, she checked out a copy of the novel to catch up on the reading. She was starting out behind. It was always harder to catch up than to keep up. She knew she would have to work twice as hard to get up to speed.

"Hey, if you need any help on anything, I'm always just a text away," the red-haired girl from her group told her. She handed Carson a sheet of paper with her cell phone number on it.

"Thanks. Emma, right?" She searched her brain to make sure she had said the right name. "I appreciate that."

She already had one new friend. Well, she wasn't a friend-friend. But at this point, even a familiar face would do. She was very different from her bestie back in her neighborhood. But at least Emma was nice. Maybe Summit Middle School wasn't going to be so bad after all.

Chapter 2

And the Winner Is

"Hey, baby. How was your first day?" her mother asked as Carson got in the car.

Her backpack was loaded with homework. She didn't make any friends. And she was tired as all get out. "Fine."

"Just fine? That's it? I've been waiting to hear about your first day. And all you have to say is fine?"

"I'm too tired for this, Mom. I walked

into school like you wanted me to. Then I went to my classes. Isn't that enough right now? Do I have to relive it?"

"Well, it couldn't have been that bad."

"It wasn't bad. It was fine, just like I said before."

They rode in silence for most of the ride home. "I'm taking you out to eat tonight. What are you in the mood for?"

"To a restaurant on a Monday?"

"My baby got accepted into an advanced school and held her own on her first day. Yes, a restaurant on a Monday." She squeezed Carson's hand, letting her know how much she loved and respected her for trying something new.

Carson tried to change her mood. She could tell that her mother was trying. Her day hadn't been *that* bad. She missed her friends. Missed having them there to joke around with during lunch, PE, after school. But overall, she could see why her mom wanted her to go to Summit.

"Well then, I'm thinking Roadhouse. Their bread and butter are calling my name!"

They had a great time together. Carson finally told her mom about her day. She told her about her project, and how all of the students were so involved. She even admitted that she could see why her mom wanted her to go there.

Her mother was pleased. Carson was happy to be able to open up to her. She had been angry for so long, but her mother was only trying to do what was best for her.

The next day when she arrived at her girls-only gym class, she was surprised that they didn't dress out. Instead, the instructors had combined their class with the boys' and set up an improvised bowling alley.

Carson loved to bowl. When her dad was around, they liked to bowl together. Since he moved to the East Coast, she hadn't bowled once. Their gym teachers went over the rules and assigned teams. The winning team would win movie tickets and free pizza coupons. It was very exciting.

She was put on a team with Mai Pham, the same Asian girl from her group in English class. She was thankful to "know" someone. The two boys on their team were Finn Franklin, who she could tell was the class clown, and Holden Smith, who seemed more serious. The teams played on their own lanes as the gym teachers kept score, posting them on a big wall for everyone to see.

When it was Carson's turn to bowl, she concentrated and sent the soft bowling ball barreling toward the pins. "Strike!" Coach T yelled as she marked her score. Her team went wild it. They were congratulating her as the sixth-grade helpers reset their pins.

"Hey, you're good," Holden told her as she rejoined them. "I'm glad you're on my team."

She could feel the blood rushing to her cheeks. She hoped he couldn't see it, though. "Thanks," she said, smiling shyly.

Mai was next up to bowl, but she missed all of the pins. "Shoot!" she said, stomping her foot. "Can you help me, Carson?"

Carson immediately went to her teammate's side, "Lead with your thumb. Point it at the pin you want to hit."

Mai sent the ball barreling toward the pins. It made contact. "Hey, that worked!" Mai was excited. "I tried that when Coach told me last week, but I wasn't so lucky."

"I guess I'm just a great teacher," Carson said proudly.

"Well, maybe you can help me," Holden responded. "Bowling just doesn't seem to be my thing."

She immediately took the bowling ball from his hands and explained what he was doing wrong. She had no idea that she had gained some unexpected haters as she helped her team maneuver through their rough spots. Holden did well with her guidance and even picked up a spare.

"You're getting better," she said, giving him a high five.

When Finn went up to bowl, he broke into a break dance, spun around, and landed a strike with little effort. Blowing his nails and wiping them on his shirt, he gave his whole team low fives, as if he was an NBA starter.

Finn's move put them in the lead. Carson was the last to bowl and got two consecutive strikes, winning the whole game for her team. Finn twirled her around. When Coach announced their win, Finn declared that Carson was their team MVP.

Carson and Mai retreated to the girls' locker room with their winning pizza coupons and movie tickets in hand.

"That was totally awesome," Mai told her. "We would never have won without— ouch!" she yelled as the same girl who Carson bumped into yesterday slammed into her. "Oh, sorry, Jessa … I must have—"

"You must have a problem! Watch where you are going next time," Jessa warned.

"Why did you apologize? She bumped into you on purpose," Carson whispered to Mai.

"You don't know yet. That's Jessa. She owns this school. It's best to stay out of her way, and that's what I intend to do."

Carson watched as Jessa's friends fussed around her. *They* even looked afraid of her. Carson had met girls like her before, maybe not as pretty or with as much money, but a bully was still a bully. She planned to stay out of her way. She didn't want their two worlds colliding. She had a feeling that hers would have the most damage.

Chapter 3

A Horse of a Different Color

Bowling had been fun and exciting. It even ended with a win for Carson's team. She talked nonstop when she arrived home. Her mother was excited that one of their favorite pastimes had landed Carson a few more friends.

"This lifetime sports class seems to be fun. Are you enjoying it?" her mom asked.

"I love it. There are so many activities

that we get to try. But I don't think anyone could go to the Olympics with the amount of time Coach spends on each one."

"But at least you get experience, right? I've never done archery before. The counselor told me that you'd be learning archery. That's pretty cool," her mom said.

"I know. I wonder what they have in store for us tomorrow," Carson said.

Well, that was yesterday. Today, she was standing next to a smelly horse that all of the other students seemed excited to see. But Carson was not. Obviously they had all met Coco before. The horse seemed just as happy to see them as they were to see her.

Carson quietly moved next to Coach T and whispered, "I don't think I'm going to be able to do this."

Coach looked surprised. "Most people are happy when Coco comes to visit."

"I'm terrified of horses," she admitted.

"Look, you're a Texan, right?" Coach T grasped her shoulder with her calloused hand. "You are going to ride this horse."

Carson looked toward Coco as the other girls were already practicing their mounts. "I'll let you start off with the mounting ramp. That should get you used to the process. The next time Coco shows up, you'll be an old pro."

Carson was doubtful and reluctant. The last thing she wanted to do was be thrown from this horse. She had heard horror stories and was not about to become a statistic.

Mai walked over to her. "What's wrong with you? You look as if you've seen a ghost or something."

"I'm scared of horses," she told her friend.

"Look, Coco is harmless. Go ahead and talk to her a little bit. You'll see."

Carson looked at Mai as if she was nuts. "I don't talk to horses."

Mai led her by the hand to where Coco was patiently allowing the other kids to mount and dismount. "Coco, this is Carson." The horse let out a neigh and bent her head a little to the side. It was like the horse wanted to cuddle. Carson was caught off guard. "I think she likes you," Mai said softly.

"Roberts!" Coach called out. "You ready to give this a go or what?"

"Or what," Carson whispered to Mai. "Sure, Coach, I'm ready."

"Did you read the entire handout that I gave you?"

"Yes, ma'am, but—"

"No buts! Get that mounting block over here."

The boys' gym coach sent Holden over to the girls' riding area to set the mounting block up for them. He gently rubbed Coco's head before turning to Carson. "Hey, you've got this." He gave her a wink as he ran back over to the boys' area.

Carson did everything that the handout said. She checked the girth of the saddle, adjusted the stirrup to her liking, put her left foot in the stirrup, and swung her right leg, kicking Coco directly on her backside.

Before she knew it, Coco took five steps forward. There was nothing underneath her body but air. She fell to the ground in mid-swing. She could hear the students gasp. Then the laughter followed from the girls. And even worse, the boys too.

Embarrassed and hurt, Carson ran to the restrooms with Mai right behind her. She could hear Coach yelling for her to get back and try again as she ran, but it was over. She would never get back on that horse or any other horse for that matter.

"Carson, slow down!" Mai yelled.

"No! That was humiliating. I want to go home. I knew that I should have never tried."

"Are you serious? That doesn't sound like you."

"You barely know me, Mai."

"You don't seem like a person who doesn't want to try. You came here in the middle of the fall semester, didn't you? That proves that you are a pretty brave girl. It was just a bad moment. You'll be fine."

Carson looked in the mirror and wiped the tears that had stained her face. She didn't want to see the other girls. She didn't feel like looking at their faces as they mocked her, so she waited them out. She knew that if she sat here, she would be late to her next class. But it was worth the tardy pass.

"Mai, you don't have to wait with me. Go to class. I don't want you to get in trouble."

"I'm not leaving you. They'll understand and give us a pass. No harm, no foul."

They heard the next bell ring. The girls' locker room had emptied out. They left the restroom and made a mad dash for their lockers. But they found nothing inside. Their lockers were empty.

Chapter 4

An Embarrassing Situation

Where are my clothes? My purse?"

"Mine are gone too," Mai said dejectedly.

"Let's see if Coach T took our stuff."

"Why would she do that?"

"I don't know," Carson said, walking toward the coach's office. They could see her prepping for her next class.

"What are you two still doing here?" she

asked in her brusque way. There was nothing soft about Coach T.

"Do you have our clothes?" Carson asked sheepishly, wishing that she didn't have to talk to this woman at all.

"No, Roberts. Why would I have your clothes?"

"Um … I … I don't know. They're gone. We don't know who took them."

"Go to the office. Let them know what happened. Then call your parents for new clothes. Or go to class in your gym clothes."

"In our gym clothes?" Mai asked. She was mortified at the thought of going through the rest of the day dressed for gym.

They walked back to the locker room. Other girls were now getting dressed out for gym. They sat down on the wooden benches and looked at each other. "What do we do?" Mai whispered to her.

"We go to class."

"Like this?" Mai asked, looking down at the blue-and-white striped jumper that she had always hated. She couldn't understand why they had to wear such ridiculous outfits. She felt like she had on a onesie. "I don't know."

"I'm not calling my mom," Carson said firmly. "She's at work. Our things will turn up at some point."

They walked down the halls, past open classroom doors. At each door they could hear laughter. They looked at each other and rolled their eyes. This was going to be a rough day.

Mai went to her class. As Carson entered her math class, she could hear the snickering. She was determined to ignore it. Even the teacher looked as if she wanted to join in. Carson walked over to her seat and sat down, pretending as if nothing was wrong. Her outsides were calm and collected, but her insides were turning flips.

"Why are you wearing that?" Emma leaned over and whispered.

Carson sat looking straight ahead and did not respond. She didn't know who had set her up to look like an idiot. She didn't know what to say, so she said nothing, vowing to find the culprit.

Just as she began the assignment, Mrs. Brooks walked over to her desk.

"Carson, may I speak with you in the hallway?"

That was the last thing Carson wanted to do. Why would Mrs. Brooks expect her to walk out in front of the whole class again? The first time was brutal enough. Her eyes pleaded with her teacher. Mrs. Brooks understood and bent down next to her desk.

"What happened? Did you soil your clothes? Is there someone who can bring you something else?"

"Someone stole everything I own. My clothes. My purse. My shoes."

"Come on. You need to go to the office."

When they entered the hallway, Mai was standing outside talking to her teacher too. Carson could tell that she had been crying. She ran to her side.

"Look, ladies. I've seen this before. It was a harmless prank," Mrs. Brooks said to them.

"Harmless? This is totally awful, terrible, embarrassing …" Carson started to raise her voice.

"Calm down, Carson. It happens every year to somebody, but it's kind of quick to make enemies so early. You just arrived on this campus, and already—"

"This is *not* my fault. I'm going to call my mother." She turned away abruptly from Mrs. Brooks and stomped down the hall. Mai was right behind her. "I can't believe she said that this was our fault," Carson fumed. Mai could see the steam rising off Carson as she made her way to the office.

Soon thereafter, Carson's mother showed up just as angry. "Are you okay?" her mother asked, grabbing her face and looking her directly in the eyes.

They sat down across from Principal Buckley.

"My daughter has already filled me in on what happened today, and I don't like it. And I really don't like that Mrs. Brooks told her it was her fault," Mrs. Roberts asserted.

"Were those her exact words?" Principal Buckley asked Carson.

"Well, no." She could see her mother's body language shift. That's what she had said on the phone to her mother. "But that's what she meant. She said it 'was a little soon to be making enemies.'"

"Well, I don't think that Mrs. Brooks meant—"

"It sounds like Carson filled in the blanks just fine. And that Coach T, don't even get me started. Telling my baby to go to class in her gym clothes." She reached over and gently touched Carson's hand. She started wondering if this was such a good idea after all. Carson had never been bullied or mistreated at her other school. And now this.

"Mrs. Brooks is one of our best teachers. What she said … She was saying it out of concern. Mrs. Roberts, we are all adjusting here. This is the first year that our student body is up to three hundred children. In some places, we are still working out the bugs. Our original student body seems to be resisting the change."

"This is more than bugs, Mrs. Buckley. I'm taking my baby home today. Her purse was stolen. She was told to go to class wearing her gym clothes. This is totally ridiculous. I don't know what kind of school you are running here." Her mother quickly stood up. "You need to get to the bottom of this. There are cameras everywhere. Surely you know who took her things. And if not, you need to. Maybe Carson would do better after you worked out the bugs in your system."

"I assure you, Ms. Roberts, this will not happen again. Carson will be fine."

Carson walked into the outer office and could hear Mai trying to explain what happened to her parents. Her mother sat quietly, looking regal.

Mai's father was furious. "What did you do? Why were these girls after you?" He looked handsome in his business suit. His features were chiseled. Mai attempted to answer his questions, but he wasn't trying to hear what she had to say. He began to speak to her in Vietnamese.

"I didn't do anything," she said in English, her head lowered. "I didn't do anything," she repeated between his rants.

She looked up only for a second as she watched Carson leave the office. "Is that her?" her father demanded. "No more. This friendship is over. Do you understand me?" he asked.

That was the last thing Carson heard as the doors to the office closed softly behind her.

Chapter 5

Pizza and a Movie

It was their little group's first weekend free. They could all hang out and be together. Carson, Mai, Finn, and Holden were an unlikely foursome as they strolled the teen-filled mall that Saturday night. They were armed with movie passes and coupons for free pizza that they won in PE. Though they didn't have to all go at the same time, they decided that being together to celebrate their victory was the best thing to do.

As they waited for their pizzas, they chatted and laughed. Finn played practical jokes on the other teenagers in the pizza parlor. He took their food when their orders were called. Normally this would upset patrons, but Finn was known for his wild pranks. They knew that he meant no harm.

"Those Carver kids need to loosen up. That guy over there almost socked me when I took his food."

"Maybe they don't want you breathing all over their pizza, Finn," Carson said, understanding their position.

"Hey, it's all good. Life's too short to care about all of that."

"You sound like you're twenty-five or something." Mai laughed. "You're only twelve years old, Finn."

"You're not talking much," Carson said, watching Holden, who was too serious for a middle school student.

"I'm always quiet. That's just how I'm made." Holden had no idea that his quiet nature made him even more appealing and mysterious to girls his age. They had been chasing him since kindergarten, and he had been running. Now he had met Carson. She seemed to be a nice girl. He liked what he knew about her so far.

Carson wasn't like the other girls at Summit. She didn't come from money. She didn't act like a snob. She was a down-to-earth girl who liked to have fun. Being with her was enough fun for him, but he didn't want her to know that. He was enjoying hanging out and getting to know her. No pressure.

"I need to go to the restroom," Carson announced. "You wanna come, Mai?"

"Sure." The girls went to freshen up before their pizza arrived.

As Carson washed her hands, she thought it would be a good time to talk to Mai. She wanted to bring up what Mr. Pham had said about her. "What did your dad say about them stealing our clothes?"

"Nothing," Mai said, looking nervous.

"Don't lie to me, Mai. I heard him tell you not to hang out with me anymore."

"I don't care what Father says about you. That wasn't your fault or mine. It was the mean girls. It's always the mean girls. Their faces change, but it's always the same at Summit."

"So do you know who did it?"

"No, but I'm sure Jessa had something to do with it. She's a pro at getting others to do her dirty work."

"Yeah. Okay, let's go. I bet our pizza is ready."

They walked out, stopping in their tracks as they watched Jessa and her friends eating their pizza and flirting with Finn and Holden.

"What are they doing?" Carson was furious. "Hey, that's our food!"

"Oh, I'm sorry. I assumed you were trying to lose weight," Jessa said to Carson as her friends erupted in laughter.

"Get some glasses, Jessa," Finn said. "Because you need them."

"Yeah, well." She turned her attention to Holden. "Hey, call me later," she said, running her fingers through his hair.

"Jessa is always so thirsty," Finn said while she was still in earshot. She turned around quickly but knew better than to respond to Finn. She was not in the mood for one of his quick-witted insults.

"I don't like her," Mai said when she was out of range.

"She's just misunderstood," Holden said, taking up for Jessa. "She does have a good side."

"Well, I have yet to see that. She's the

41

spawn of the devil. Those girls following her are her evil minions." Mai watched the entourage as they all sashayed behind Jessa, hanging on her every word. "It's been this way our entire lives."

"Did you two used to go out?" Carson asked Holden.

He shook his head. "She lives across the street from me. We used to play together. If there were such thing as arranged marriages in Texas, I'd probably wind up with her. She hasn't had it as easy as people think. I feel sorry for her sometimes."

"I want to toss her in a garbage can sometimes," Finn said, looking away toward the door and getting a laugh from the table.

"Hey, let's go to the movie. I hate being late," Carson warned.

They had the best time that night. Mai was the happiest of them all. She had never hung out with Finn or Holden. It took Carson coming to their school for them to even know her name. Now she felt as though she actually had friends.

Mai didn't care what her parents thought of Carson and her meager background. She made Mai fun, unafraid, and bold. Characteristics that she had hidden for a long time. Now she felt as though people were starting to see a different side of her.

"Thank you so much for coming to Summit. I don't know where you've been my whole life."

"On the other side of town!" Carson yelled as she got into her mom's car. "It's okay … I'm here now. Bye!"

"Well, you look like you are having fun," Carson heard a voice say from the back seat. It was Jody, her best friend.

"Hey, baby," her mom said. "Jody asked to ride with me to pick you up."

Carson immediately climbed into the

back seat with Jody, looped her arm through hers, and rode that way all the way home. She caught her up on all of her drama: the locker scandal, mean girl Jessa, quiet boy Holden, class clown Finn, Coco the horse.

Jody laughed with her at the funny parts and got mad when Carson got mad. She was truly her best friend.

They pulled up in front of Carson's house. Carson and Jody stayed outside, talking on the front porch swing. "Do you think that Holden likes you?" Jody asked her.

"Why would you say that?" Carson asked, surprised.

"It just sounds like he does. He could have gone to the mall, pizza, and movies with anybody. I think he wanted to go with you."

"I don't know. I guess. It's hard to tell anything with Holden. And Jessa lives across the street from him. There's history there, but I don't know the whole story."

"Yeah, well, be careful of that one. She reminds me of Ranisha at Carver. Jealousy is a dangerous thing. She may have even been the one who took your clothes."

"Yeah. You may be right. But at least we got our stuff back the next day. You know, Mai and Emma think the same thing about Jessa."

"Well, they're probably right. I can't wait to meet them."

"You may have to. I forgot to mention that Mai's father hates me. She's sneaking around to hang out with me."

"Wow, you have made quite an impression at SMS." Jody laughed. She wished she could be there. Together, they would rule those preppy kids.

Chapter 6

Another Wounded Soul

Carson was late for class again. It seemed to be the story of her life since arriving at Summit. She was still getting used to her new surroundings. She entered the restroom knowing she would have to get another pass from the office. She figured that they would cut her off at some point, but they seemed to be tolerant of her situation. She dashed into the second stall.

She could hear someone in the stall next

to her. It sounded like she was crying. She could hear sniffles.

She whispered, "Are you okay?" But there was no response from the stall. "Hey, it can't be that bad. I'm here if you want to talk."

She exited her own stall, washed her hands, and opened the restroom door. She didn't leave the restroom, though. Instead, she stayed there, ready to be someone's shoulder to cry on. She had been there. It wasn't fun handling drama by yourself.

Before she knew it, she was face-to-face with Jessa. *I should have walked out when I had the chance,* she thought.

"You waited? You wanted to see me like this? Was this all your little plan?" Jessa was coming toward Carson like she was ready to let her have it.

"Jessa, I didn't know it was you in the stall. Honestly, I probably wouldn't have reached out like I did. I don't want to get in your business. Later." She turned to walk out of the restroom.

"Wait!" Jessa cried, wiping the tears from her face. "I *could* use someone to talk to."

Carson took a deep breath before turning around to face the girl who had made middle school hell for so many people. She remembered what Holden had said, "She's just misunderstood."

"Okay, shoot," Carson told her as they leaned against the window of the restroom.

"I think it's divorce time in the McCain household."

"Why do you think that?"

"My parents had an argument this morning. All over some lady from his job."

"Do you think that he's cheating on your mom?"

"I don't know what to think. Are *your* parents still together?"

Carson had not planned on telling her anything about her own life. She was there to listen, not share. "No, they aren't together," she said, remembering a time when she felt just like Jessa. The fairy tale was long over for her.

"Was it hard for you?"

This was a little too much. "Let's just say that it gets easier. You get your own routine. It's different. It's not better or worse, just different," she lied. She was still hurting, but it wasn't something she would tell just anyone. She definitely wasn't about to tell Jessa.

"Well, maybe we could hang out some time. I really need a friend right now."

"Jessa, you have plenty of friends."

"Yeah, and none of them understand me. They think that this package is all there is. I'm more than a pretty face. I feel too."

Maybe she was on the up and up. Carson

was afraid that she had judged Jessa too quickly. Too harshly. In this moment, maybe she was seeing the real Jessa, the one who hurt just like everyone else.

"Okay, Friday night. Let's hang. You can come over after school."

Carson was happy that they had finally come to some workable arrangement. She hated making enemies. It just wasn't her thing. She would rather have peace. Now Jessa was coming to her house on Friday. She would be the first person Carson entertained at home from her new school.

When Carson got in her mom's car on Friday, she knew that she had made a mistake. Jessa was used to riding around in her mom's Range Rover or her dad's Mercedes, not a beat-up old Honda Accord.

Jessa was on the way to the car. No DVD. No satellite radio. No navigation. It was embarrassing. Jessa jumped in the back seat, greeted Mrs. Roberts politely, and they were ready to go.

Not as painful as I thought, Carson thought to herself. Allowing Jessa to see their home didn't seem so bad.

"We'll be in my room, Mom," Carson yelled as soon as they walked through the door.

"Can I get you girls a snack?" She could tell that her mother was excited she was making friends at Summit. But Carson was still trying to wrap her brain around the fact that the most popular girl in school was at her house. She hadn't told anyone that Jessa was coming over, not even Emma or Mai. They would surely call her a fool.

"We will get something later, Mom. Don't worry about us." She turned her attention back to Jessa, who was looking at old pictures and learning way more about her family than she would have liked. "What do you like to do?" Carson asked her.

"I just listen to music and zone out at home." She studied one picture from Carson's dresser. "Is this your dad?" she asked. Carson nodded her head. "My parents are a trip, Carson. You have no clue. Sometimes I just want to escape all their drama. I go to my friends' houses in the neighborhood. I'm never home anymore. When I am, I try to stay invisible."

"What do they think about that?" Carson asked her. Even during her parents' hardest years, they made sure their daughter always came first.

"They couldn't care less. They don't even know that I'm over here now. I'll text my mom and let her know when she can come and get me."

Wow! Carson thought. She thought that Jessa had it all, but now she realized that she had her all wrong. Her house was bigger. Her car was bigger. But so were her problems. Her little two-bedroom house and single-parent family didn't seem so bad after all.

They were interrupted by a knock on her bedroom door. It was Jody. "Hey, darling. You free?" she asked half-knocking and half-entering.

Jessa looked like she had seen a ghost as Jody entered in her basketball shorts and freshly Bantu-knotted hair. It made Carson's heart smile, but she could tell that her guest was uncomfortable.

Jessa didn't say a word until Jody spoke to her. "What's up? Who are you?"

"Me, oh, nothing. I mean … I'm Jessa," she said, visibly shaken. She was a long way from her beachfront property. She was on Carson's turf and starting to feel it.

"Oh, so *you're* Jessa. I've heard a lot about you," Jody said, dripping sarcasm.

"Oh?" Jessa looked worried. She knew that it couldn't be good.

"Carson, can I talk you for a second in private?" Carson and Jody walked out to the front yard. "What in the heck is *Jessa* doing in your bedroom?"

"I'm just helping her through some things. That's all."

"I'm not buying it at all. Just be careful. There's something in her eyes. That girl is trouble."

"Everyone says that. She's just misunderstood." She was starting to sound like Holden.

"I'm not buying that."

"Carson!" her mother yelled out the front door. She knew that look.

"Hey, I better go. We'll talk. Don't worry about me. I'm a big girl."

"Yeah, I'm bigger. Make sure she knows that she has to deal with me if anything happens to you."

They gave each other their signature dap and parted ways.

"Don't be rude to your guest," her mother whispered, ushering her back into the house.

She walked into her room just as Jessa was shutting down Carson's Friender page. She looked guilty. She had been caught red-handed.

Chapter 7

Let Me Tell You

Were you logged on to my Friender account?" Carson asked through narrowed eyes.

"Why would I be on *your* Friender account? I was checking my messages. I was just letting my mom know where to come and pick me up. I gave her your address. Is that okay with you?"

Carson could tell that Jessa was offended. She didn't mean to accuse her of anything sinister. But after talking to Jody, she was a little more guarded. Now she felt bad for making her guest uneasy.

"My bad, Jessa … it's just, people keep warning me about being friends with you."

Jessa eyes began to fill with tears. "Seriously, people treat me like I slap babies or something. Why do they always assume the worst about me?"

"I don't think that you're bad. That wasn't fair of me. I'm sorry."

"No worries. What's up with those snacks your mom was talking about."

"Good idea. Let's go raid the kitchen." They found a tray of croissant sandwiches, cookies, cupcakes, and fruit. It looked as though a deli had just delivered their goodies.

"Your mom is the truth!" Jessa said, looking at the spread Mrs. Roberts had prepared.

They took their food to the bedroom. Carson introduced Jessa to some of her favorite music on MyTube. They tried to do the latest dances but wound up looking like they were in pain. They laughed at their reflections in the mirror so hard they both tumbled over on Carson's bed.

Just as they recovered from their fit of laughter, the doorbell rang. It was Mrs. McCain. She looked like Malibu Barbie, perfectly tanned.

She was different from the woman Carson had pictured in her head. She looked like she didn't have a care in the world. The huge diamond on her finger looked as though it would cause her hand to cramp from its weight.

She wore white shorts and a flowing blouse that probably came from a fancy boutique. A place Carson's mother could only dream about shopping at. She was the picture of perfection and looked completely out of place in the Roberts's home.

When she spoke, she sounded like a real-life Texas girl, the kind depicted on the big screen. Her Southern drawl was enchanting. "Mrs. Roberts, thank you so much for letting Jessa come over. I wish she would have let me know, though." She shot Jessa a glance.

Jessa rolled her eyes, dismissing her mother's disapproval. "Hey, call me later this weekend," she said to Carson. "We're going to hang out at the mall if you want to join us."

"That'd be awesome!" Carson was so excited. She couldn't believe Jessa and her friends wanted to hang out with *her*. Even back at her old school, she wasn't in the popular clique. She had her core four and no more. But now she was venturing into unfamiliar territory.

The girls hugged each other. Carson could see her mom's elation when they left. "Oh my goodness, Carson. That's why I sent you to SMS. Do you see how doors are just going to fly open for you? Those are the types of friends you need. I really like Jessa. Her mom is so beautiful."

"Yeah, Jessa said she used to be a Dallas Cowboys cheerleader back in the day. She didn't seem too stuck-up by it, though."

"Jessa's dad basically runs Texsun City. He's the plant manager at the largest refinery out here, Texsun Oil. Imagine you working there, my baby."

"Mom, you are way over-the-top. You just met Jessa."

"I just want the best for you," her mom replied.

Carson retreated to her room. So much had happened in the past few days. Now she was actually going to hang out at the mall with the school It Girls. It was like she was living a dream or something. She just wished her mother would slow down on planning her future.

The next day she got dropped off at the mall for her fun day. She texted Jessa to see where she was. But she never received a reply. She searched the usual hangouts by the theater, food court, and arcade. But Jessa and her crew were nowhere to be found.

Carson tried calling Jessa's phone, but she went straight to voice mail. Just when she had given up, she spotted Jessa and her friends walking around, giggling with some boys Carson didn't recognize.

"Jessa!" she yelled, waving.

"Hey, Carson! I thought you were supposed to meet up with us an hour ago."

"I've been texting and calling you for nearly an hour."

"Oh? I didn't get anything." She opened her gray cell phone case covered with bling. "Aw, look. I did get a couple of messages. We were having so much fun. I must not have heard."

Carson could see all of Jessa's friends laughing behind her. Monroe was the first to speak, "Come on, Jessa. We're going to miss the movie."

"Hold on. Geez!" She rolled her eyes and turned back to Carson. "You want to come to the movie with us?"

"I didn't bring enough money. My mom will be here in about thirty minutes."

"All fixable. My treat. Text your mom and let her know that the movie lets out at nine thirty. Cool?"

Carson smiled. "Sure! Let's go."

Carson sat between Monroe and Harper in the theater. She thought that Jessa would sit next to her, but she was on the far end. Neither Monroe nor Harper paid any attention to her. She felt left out as they laughed at the movie and cracked private jokes across her lap.

Seriously, I should have just gone home.

When the movie was over, she'd had enough. Then Jessa rushed up and grabbed her. "Wasn't that awesome? I want a boyfriend just like Cash. He was to die for."

"He was a cutie," Carson admitted. She was still salty that Jessa didn't sit by her. But how could she stay mad when Jessa was so excited? "Hey, my mom's already out front. I'll catch up with you later."

She ran ahead to get in the car but could hear someone calling her name. "Carson! Carson!" She turned around to find Holden smiling widely. "Did you just come out of the theater?"

"Yeah," she said, looking to see if Jessa could see her. She didn't want her new friend getting mad at her again.

"That part when Cash pulled that practical joke on—"

She cut him off abruptly. She wanted to get far away from him before Jessa walked out. "Hey, my mom's right there. I have to run."

"Okay. Call me later!" he yelled

She was horrified. Monroe and Harper were coming out of the door just as Holden yelled. They looked at her as if she had just committed the ultimate sin. Jessa, Tyson, and Drew were right behind them. She could tell that they were filling Jessa in on what they had heard. The five girls peered at Carson as she got into her mom's car.

"Did you have fun?" her mother asked excitedly.

"I don't want to talk about it, Mom. Please just drive." Her mother could tell that something had happened. But she respected Carson's wishes and drove home in silence.

On Monday morning, Carson didn't know what to expect. She didn't know where she stood with Jessa. She had to confess to

Mai and Emma that she had been hanging out with the enemy. Everything was so messed up. Her mind didn't know how to process it all. She didn't know where to begin. She was an emotional wreck and getting more anxious by the minute.

"Hey, Carson! Wait up," Emma said, joining her at their lockers.

"Hey," Carson responded dryly.

"You okay? You didn't say a lot in English class."

"Yeah, sorry. I just had a long weekend. That's all."

"Okay, text me later if you can. These teachers are cracking down on our cell phones. So be careful."

"Always," she said to her friend, giving her a small grin. It was all she could muster.

Her next class was with Mai. She knew she would question her about the weekend. She didn't want to talk about it. She didn't know what to say. Just as she predicted, that was the first question Mai asked. It almost made Carson blow a fuse.

"What's the big deal about the weekend? Why is everyone asking me that?"

Mai looked confused. "I was just asking. I guess it didn't go well."

"Ugh. Just stop talking to me, Mai. It's all too much right now."

Mai turned away from her friend, a little bit hurt and a whole lot confused. She knew that Carson would talk about it when she was ready. She definitely wasn't going to push. This was a new Carson. She almost didn't recognize her at all.

They sat at lunch in silence. Carson, Mai, and Emma picked at their food and tried not to address the obvious issue that was between them.

Finally, Emma broke the silence. "So, Mai, how was your weekend?"

Mai looked nervously from Emma to Carson and shook her head.

"It's okay, Mai," Carson told her. "I wanted to talk to y'all about it anyway. It's killing me."

"What?" they said in unison, moving in closer to their friend. Finally, she was going to put their suspicions to rest. She told them everything: the encounter in the restroom, Jessa coming over, Jody's suspicions, finding Jessa snooping on her computer, the mall, the movies.

"Why did you trust her? Why didn't you talk to me first?" Emma asked.

Just as Mai was about to chime in, Jessa rounded the corner. "Hey, Carson." She took a seat right at their table. All of her friends stood around them. "So, did you ever call Holden like he asked you to?" She took a french fry from Carson's plate and ate it.

"No."

"Why? I know you wanted to. I see how you drool all over him."

"That is not true," Carson protested. "We are just friends." She wasn't even interested in boys in that way. He was just a cool kid. She enjoyed hanging out. Carson couldn't understand what the big deal was.

"It's no biggie anyways. I'm totally over him. I just wanted you to know that. Plus, I like hanging out with you more than him any day. So, whatever. Call me later."

They watched as the lionesses walked away, sauntering through the cafeteria as if they owned it.

"Don't trust her, Carson," Emma said, still keeping her eyes on Jessa. "I heard that she was the one who got her crew to take your clothes in PE."

"I don't believe that. Why would she do that? You heard what she said. She likes hanging out with me."

"And you believe her?" Mai asked. "No way. I'm with Emma. She is the only one mean enough to carry it out."

"Y'all are just jealous because she wants to hang out with me and not you," Carson spat at them. She had used her words to hurt them, and she hoped it worked. They were trying to hurt her, and she was angry. She pushed herself away from the table and quickly left the cafeteria. She could see Jessa as she flew past her. Jessa's girls started laughing and looked back over at Emma and Mai.

"Poor Carson, she's dancing with the devil," Emma said, remembering the torture that those mean girls had put her through. It had been years ago, when she was just like Carson, trying to fit in. But it still stung.

"Yeah, but some things you have to learn on your own," Mai announced as they stood to leave for the second half of the day.

Chapter 8

A Familiar Face

Later that evening, Carson let her friends' words sink into her spirit. It was all she could think about. After being around Jessa, she was sure the two of them were okay. There was something nagging her, though. Something about Jessa thinking that Carson was drooling all over Holden.

Why would she say that?

If that was the way Jessa saw it, then she

was harboring negative feelings somewhere deep.

Carson fell back on her bed and turned the TV off. She couldn't think about it anymore. The only person she knew who would be real with her was Jody. She walked across the street and knocked on Jody's bedroom window.

She could see her friend engrossed in the Disney Channel's newest show. Jody never took her eyes off the television as she crossed the room to raise the window for Carson. It was like they were little kids all over again.

"What's up?" Jody asked her as she sat on the bed. "You only use the window now when something's wrong."

"That's not true."

Jody gave her a knowing look and asked again, "What's up?"

"I don't even know where to begin. You know Jessa came over the other day, right?"

"Uh-huh." Her expression read, "I told

you so." Jody sensed that Jessa would be the cause of her friend's troubles.

"Well, number one, I went to the movies with her and her friends. First, Jessa leaves me looking all over the mall for them. Then when we get in the movie, I'm sandwiched between Harper and Monroe. They acted like I wasn't even there.

After the movie, Holden's outside. They see us talking and hear him tell me to call him. By the time I get to lunch today, Jessa is in my face saying that I like Holden. Says I can have him. I'm so emotional by this time that I wind up snapping at Mai and Emma. Now it's like I have no friends."

"One thing you will always have is a friend. I got you, so don't ever worry about that."

"I know, Jody. But you are not at Summit with me. I can't be a one-girl show."

"Look, you messed up with your day

ones. That's fixable. I already warned you about Jessa. You didn't want to listen. That girl is trouble. She's dangling her friendship in your face like someone dangles a carrot in front of a horse."

"Can we skip the horse analogies right now?"

Jody started laughing. "I forgot about the horse incident. My bad."

Carson had to laugh too. It was funny looking back on it. But nobody could have told her that on the day she kicked Coco and was sent flying through the air.

"What I was trying to say was stop trusting Jessa," Jody said. "She is not your friend. I don't know how to put it more plainly than that. Make it right with Emma and Mai. They wouldn't last a day at Carver, but they sound like cool girls."

"Yeah, you are right, Jody. I don't know what I'd do without you."

Carson left the way she came. The October night air was getting more brisk with the setting sun. The wind swept through the fabric of her robe. She shivered against the breeze as she climbed in through her own window.

She went to the kitchen to make hot chocolate and focus on her math homework. If she hadn't talked to Jody, she knew that she would have never been able to get anything done. How could you get your homework done when you have friendships in trouble?

Chapter 9

The Mask Is Off

The next morning at their lockers was awkward. You could cut the tension with a knife. This was no way for the three of them to start their day. It was homecoming week. Who wanted to be fighting with their two best school friends during homecoming?

Mai and Emma didn't even talk to each other, afraid that they would make Carson angry. Each shut her locker. Then they headed in the direction of the one class they all shared together, English.

"Hey, can we talk before first period starts? Let's talk in the restroom. I won't keep you long," Carson pleaded. Emma and Mai looked at each other. They both felt burned from the last time they saw each other. She saw their hesitation. "Please," she begged.

Mai and Emma turned toward the nearest girls' restroom for some privacy.

"Talk, Carson. What do you want from us?" Mai asked. Carson could see that she was angry.

"Look, this isn't easy. I messed up. I'm sorry. You two are the ones I love. The ones I want a real friendship with."

"You got caught up in their hype. I know you did," Emma said. "They did the same thing to me back in fifth grade. They invited me to one of their slumber parties. They pretty much made that night miserable for me. I was so embarrassed. I didn't even call my mom. As soon as the sun came up, I was out of there."

"Oh, Em, I had no idea."

"I'm over it now. I just didn't want the same thing to happen to you," Emma said, choking back tears from the awful memory. Mai was quick to grab her hand.

"Let me say this. It will never happen again," Carson vowed.

Mai was a harder sell. "It better not. I'm going against my father's wishes to be your friend. This is how you treat me? I thought you had my back. Just like I have yours."

"And I do. If I spend the rest of junior high proving it to you, I will." The bell rang. That was their signal. They hurried next door to their class on time, no passes needed.

That night Carson lay happily on her bed. Her friendships were back on track. Her homework was complete. And she was on her MyTube page, listening to some new music. Life was good. She could hear her cell phone ringing.

Who is interrupting my flow?

To her surprise, it was Holden. He never called her, even though he'd had her number since they all went to the mall. She had done her best to avoid him and Jessa. She wanted out of their little love triangle. She ignored the call and sent him to voice mail. She did not check her messages. Five minutes later, her phone rang again.

What could be so urgent?

"Hello?" she snapped.

"Hey, Carson. It's me, Holden."

"I know. What's up, Holden?"

"Are you okay? You sound funny."

"I'm fine. What do you want?"

"I was wondering if you would mind helping me out with the essay that we're writing in English. It seems to have me stumped."

"You need to find somebody else. I can't help you." Then she just hung up on him. Nothing like a dose of she's just not that into you. She felt bad for hurting his feelings. But she didn't need drama in her life.

The next day she avoided the normal routes. She didn't want to run into Holden. She ignored him in English. But after lunch, he was standing by her locker, waiting for her. She felt trapped.

Emma and Mai were walking with her, laughing about something. There was a small opening in the crowded hallway. She could see Jessa was coming toward her with all of her followers in tow. She looked from them to Holden to her two friends. It was as if everything was going in slow motion. She couldn't warn her friends fast enough.

Before she knew it, they were all in front of her locker. Holden's gaze was fixed on her. He reached out and grabbed her hand. She tried to pull away before anyone could see. But it was too late.

"You don't have to pretend for my sake," Jessa spat, getting right in Carson's face. "I know you like him. Just admit it."

"You're making a fool out of yourself, Jessa," Holden said quickly. "I told you the two of us would never be more than friends. You're more like a sister to me." Holden was trying to diffuse the situation.

"Shut up, Holden. This isn't about you. It's about the fact that I befriended her! Carson. Pitiful little friendless, fatherless, money-less girl. I even went to that raggedy little shack you call a house. I drove around in that wretched death trap of a car. Teaches me to go slumming. I see why your father ditched you and started a new family. I would have too."

They were drawing a crowd. The larger the audience, the more vicious Jessa became.

"Let's get to class!" They could hear the vice principal's voice getting closer and closer.

Carson couldn't move. She wanted to cry. But she couldn't give Jessa and her minions the satisfaction.

Emma and Mai were shocked. It was like watching a train wreck. The best thing they could do was pull Carson away from the drama. Holden tried to get to her too. But he could only watch as she was dragged away.

He looked back at Jessa and saw the real girl for the first time. The person who others knew. "Jessa, you are mean and heartless. Never come to my house again. How would you feel if I outted your family's dirty laundry?"

"But, Holden!" His words stung. He was her friend, not Carson's. That little nobody had come to Summit and turned her true love against her. "She's gonna pay," Jessa vowed to her friends as Holden walked away, leaving her looking like a fool.

Chapter 10

My Truth

With Jessa's words ringing in her head, Carson wanted out of there. She wanted to be far away from Summit. Far away from the sea of students who looked at her, thinking that they knew who she really was. She ran down the hallway. She didn't care about her last class, or the fact that she would be marked absent. She wanted—needed—to be alone.

Mai and Emma didn't look as if they

were going to give her that space. They were hot on her heels, yelling her name.

"Stop, Carson!" It was Mai. The hallways were emptying. There was nowhere to hide. She found herself close to the auditorium. She darted in before they gained more gawkers.

"Carson, please," Emma pleaded with her, following her into the empty auditorium.

Carson slumped down into the nearest seat. She let the waterfall of tears flow.

Mai was on one side of her and Emma was on the other. She could feel her friends' hands as they gently stroked her back.

"Don't worry about her, Carson. She makes up things about everyone. It's what she does," Emma said, trying to console her.

But Jessa hadn't made up any of it. She had described Carson's world with pinpoint accuracy. She had even nailed the feelings Carson had each time she visited her father's new home.

"She didn't lie. She didn't make it up. It's all true."

"Oh, Carson. Don't say that." Mai's voice cracked.

"It is true, but I never confided in her. How would she know those things? I've never even told my mom. The only person who knows is Jody, and she would never tell a soul."

"I don't understand."

"When I was in New Jersey at my dad's, I told Jody everything about his new house, new baby, new wife. How I didn't feel that I belonged there. I wanted to come home, but I didn't. Jody talked me into sticking it out. And I did."

Emma handed Carson a tissue.

"Finally at the end of my trip, my dad and I had a talk. I felt a bit better. But I knew my life had changed. No matter how much he reassured me that I would always be his little girl, I knew that he had turned a corner." Carson sniffed. Dabbed her eyes. "The good news is that we are working on our relationship. Each day it gets a little better. I still feel sorry for myself from time to time. But Mom and I are getting our happy back."

Emma's wheels were turning. "So how did Jessa know?"

"What?" Carson's senses were in overdrive. "I don't know," she said slowly. Then the scene played out like a movie. She watched herself enter her bedroom. She watched as Jessa clicked off her Friender page. It was like a bad dream. Jessa hadn't been talking to her mom at all. She had been looking at Carson's most private conversations. "Oh my … " her hand covered her mouth.

"What?" Mai asked.

"What's wrong? Say something, Carson," said Emma.

"She knows *everything*."

"What's everything?" the girls asked in unison.

Carson's eyes went from Mai to Emma. She wanted to put those painful months of being homeless behind her. She wanted to separate all of those awful memories from her new reality. She hadn't wanted to come to Summit. But starting fresh was the only thing that gave her the courage to try. She began to tell her friends of her father's other relationship. Of how he had chosen that woman over her mother.

She told them how they had been left in a big empty house. How the constables had come and kicked them out. With nowhere to go and only the few belongings that they were able to load in their car, they left their home. The neighborhood had watched. Some from their windows. Some from their lawns.

Other women hoped they would never have to deal with this. Carson's neighborhood friends cried. They lived with her mom's friends. Charity. Sometimes they had a private room. Sometimes they slept on an air mattress in the living room.

That was before her mom went to court. Before the child support they so desperately needed. She had been left fatherless, homeless, and penniless. The only place that felt normal to her was Friender. She could tell Jody everything, play by play, as the nightmare unfolded. She had never erased those conversations or visited that thread again. But it was there. And now Jessa had found it.

"She's going to ruin me. What she said in that hallway was only the tip of the iceberg. She knows my deepest, darkest secrets."

"We won't give her the pleasure of ruining you," Emma said defiantly. "Her path of destruction has gone on long enough. This time, Jessa won't win."

They came up with a plan. Jessa didn't

have Summit's students fooled. They were afraid of her. It was the teachers. The principal. That's who was fooled. With a plan in place, they were going to expose Jessa. She was conniving, backstabbing, cruel, and heartless. And now everyone would know.

There was one thing they could count on. Jessa would always seek revenge. Especially if she was backed into a corner.

Chapter 11

Sharpened Words

The next morning, Carson wanted nothing more than to stay home and escape the stares and whispers that were sure to follow her all day. She'd lie in bed all day. But she knew her mother would be in her room soon to wake her up.

Pretend to have a headache? Or face the music?

Knowing that skipping school would only postpone what was coming, she reluctantly got out of bed. She could hear the soft knock on the door as she brushed her teeth.

"Carson, it's time to get—oh, you're already up?"

"Yes, ma'am. I'll be done in a minute."

"Good. I don't want you to miss the bus."

Carson washed her face, splashing herself with cold water. It helped her think. She played out the bus ride to school. The looks from students who thought they knew something about her. Then putting the plan into action. She dried her face and willed herself to move. She couldn't stay here all day. She had to expect the unexpected and stay strong.

She sat down at the table filled with her morning favorites: fried Zummo's sausages, eggs, and toast. Her mother always sent her to school with a hot breakfast. But today the food felt odd in her mouth. She had no appetite as nerves overwhelmed her.

"Mom, can I ask you something?"

"Of course," she said, joining her daughter at their kitchen table.

"How did you deal with everyone knowing about Dad leaving us? I mean, when you had to go back to work and all."

"It wasn't easy. But I knew that I had to rip the bandage off. Face it head on."

"But what was it like? Ripping it off."

"It hurt, but I got through it. And you will too."

Carson's questions had given her away. It was as if her mother had super powers and could read her mind. She looked down at her breakfast. It was getting cold. "I thought I could start over. New school, new me. You know?"

"That's the funny thing about the past. It has a way of sneaking its way into the present. Carson, it's not your fault what happened between your dad and me. I'm sorry that it hurt you. But we got through it and still kept a smile on our faces. Together, we can make it through anything. Don't worry, baby. Life has a way of working itself out."

Carson, Mai, and Emma were determined that life would work itself out in their favor. Mai and Emma had witnessed Jessa and her friends tip the scales of justice. Because of Jessa's dad's influence, they seemed to get away with everything. But if the two girls had anything to do with it, this time would be different.

Carson walked through the hallways, keeping her head straight. She ignored the gossip. She had anticipated it.

"You all right?" Emma asked.

"I'm okay."

"Hey, here comes Holden. See you in class." Emma gave her friend a knowing nod and headed off to first period.

"Hey, I tried to call you," he said as he arrived at her locker.

"I know. It was just … "

"Don't worry about it. So you change your mind yet on helping me out with that project?"

She turned around to meet his gaze. She wasn't sure if their plan would work. After Jessa had humiliated her, she was sure that Holden wouldn't even want to be around her. But he proved that he was a good guy just by standing there and talking to her.

"You still want to hang out? After all of that?"

"You act like you were at fault. That was Jessa's doing. I've never seen that side of her, but I guess I knew it was there. I've heard the stories too many times."

"Yeah." Out of the corner of her eye, she could see the mean girls walking toward her. Jessa's entourage numbered more girls than usual. Carson's heart began to pound fast and loud. She tried to keep her cool, but her body tensed up, sensing that trouble was inevitable.

The all-girl crew laughed in unison as Jessa whispered. They looked Carson's way. Some pointed at her, as if she were a circus act.

"Don't let them get to you," Holden said, grabbing her hand. "I'm going to walk you to class. I'll be at the door when class is over. I'll make sure she leaves you alone."

"Okay," she agreed. They walked to class hand in hand. It was the first time a boy had held her hand so publicly. They had witnesses. Kids weren't trying to hide their surprised looks.

Just like he promised, Holden was at the door when class ended. He was there before she could gather her belongings. "Holden, you are so sweet. You don't have to do this."

"I feel that I'm somewhat to blame. Every girl who gets close to me winds up on Jessa's hit list. I called her out on it before. It's happened in our neighborhood too. She always plays innocent, like it's their fault. But this time I saw it with my own eyes."

The tardy bell rang, signaling the need to hurry to their next class. They parted ways at the classroom door.

Holden escorted her to her classes for the entire week. He also walked her to her bus at the end of the day. Every day.

By Friday, the three girls felt the need to regroup. They ate the square cafeteria pizza while trying to shift their plan into full speed.

"Look, this plan isn't working. I'm being eaten alive on Friender. I can't put out the fires fast enough. I'm becoming the laugh-ingstock of this school. Jessa is not affected in the least by my relationship with Holden. Maybe she really doesn't like him anymore."

"I'm telling you," Emma said. "She will show her hand at some point. Just do what you are doing."

"I feel bad for leading Holden on."

"Carson, I hate to break it to you, but there are worse things than spending time with Holden. Before you came here, Holden was everybody's secret crush. 'I heart Holden' is found in just about every diary in this school," Mai lectured. "You bet I had a crush too. The boy is hot!"

Emma laughed. "Guilty!" she admitted. "I put it in my journal too!"

Carson could not understand why he would be interested in her if so many girls had been chasing him. "Well, what does he want with me?"

"Have you looked in a mirror lately?"

Emma asked her. "You are a cute girl. Smart. Funny."

"And African American. You are new to Holden's world. I think he's liking what he's seeing," Mai added.

Carson thought about her own looks. She felt discarded since her father left. When she was younger, she knew she was cute. Now she wasn't so sure. If she was all that, then her father would still be in Texas and not across the country.

Holden appeared out of nowhere to escort her to class. At lunch he sat down at a table and waited for the bell. When it rang, he grabbed her hand and walked in the direction of her class.

He was even there after the last class of the day. It was Friday. He wouldn't see her all weekend. But he wanted to spend some time with her. Instead of their usual hangout by the bike racks, Carson steered them to the picnic tables to wait for the buses to load. She knew that would put them front and center. Right in Jessa's line of sight.

They said to put the plan into overdrive.

As he sat down on the table, she looped her pinky finger through his and leaned away from him. He pulled her into him and whispered in her ear. She began to laugh. But she stopped and watched Jessa coming toward them. She was followed by an even larger group of girls. They seemed eager to watch Jessa send Carson home in tears before the weekend.

"Well, well, well, if it isn't the prince and the pauper."

"What do you want, Jessa?" Holden asked, trying to get rid of her. Carson had a different plan.

"Jessa, go away. You want what I have. You are just jealous." She turned her back on the entourage and went back to her conversation with Holden. To her, the mean girl was invisible. She surprised everyone by standing up for herself with her obvious diss. Not many people had the courage to mess with Jessa.

"You turn around and look at me when I'm talking to you. Or I'll embarrass you both out here," she warned.

"Jessa, go!" Holden demanded. "Just leave her alone."

"No, she's the one who pretended to be my friend. She knew I liked you. But she went after you anyway. I'm the one you should be consoling, not her. She's trash!"

Carson turned around to face her enemy. She could see the hatred in Jessa's eyes. She had never been disliked so much or so publicly.

"That's right," Jessa spat. "You were thrown away just like trash! You are a home-less, begging squatter! Where's your Will Work for Food sign? Holden deserves better than you. But don't worry, he'll tire of you. Just. Like. Daddy."

Carson moved to get closer to her. Holden held her back.

"What? You gonna hit me? Is that how you do it in yo' hood?" She laughed and her entourage laughed too.

The plan wasn't working. Where was the principal? The vice principal didn't come over either. Emma and Mai were nowhere in sight. She had stood up for herself. But now everyone was laughing louder.

She shook herself from Holden's grasp and boarded the crowded school bus. Luckily, the first row was still vacant. She slumped down in the seat. She felt defeated and alone. With nowhere to turn, she closed her eyes and let her head rest against the window.

He'll tire of you. Just ... like ... Daddy. She shook her head, as if this would stop the automatic replay. It didn't work.

Chapter 12

In Your Face

Carson had attempted to stand up for herself. But there were too many of them. Jessa was too powerful at this school. She was thinking about a different plan now, one to get her away from this awful place. From Holden. From Jessa.

When the bus rounded the corner, she knew she could no longer see Summit. She opened her eyes. She stared out the window. A tear rolled down her cheek. She quickly wiped it away.

Be strong, she commanded herself. *Where were Mai and Emma? This was their stupid idea anyway. The plan totally failed.*

They were dropped off in the crowded mall parking lot each day. Carson got off the bus and looked for her mom's car. She heard a car's horn and saw her mother in a convertible Mustang, waving her hand like crazy.

"Do you like it? Mom got us a new car."

"How can we afford this?" she asked her mother glumly.

"Since when do you worry about my bank account? We are fine. Now let's take a drive across the bridge."

The wind seemed to blow away the difficult week. It was still fall, but it felt more like summer. A warm front had swept through Texsun City. It was a wonderful day to enjoy a drive. Carson looked at her mother's carefree smile. It was contagious. They pulled over at one of the food trucks by the pier. After ordering hot dogs and cheese fries, they watched the ships being guided into the harbor by barges.

"So how was it?" her mother asked, reading her daughter's body language. "How did it go?" Carson knew that she was referring to their conversation earlier in the week. She hated to tell her mother what she was going through at school. She didn't want her to worry.

"It was hard, like you said." She twirled her fry in the cheese before taking a bite.

"Hey, look at is this way. You don't have to worry about it coming out anymore. It's done. It can't be done again."

Carson knew that her mother was right. Jessa had used every piece of information she had. But Carson was still standing.

"Now you just heal. Mama is slowly trying to piece our lives back together. You have to find a way to do the same."

They rode back over the bridge as the sun started to set. The once warm temperature was turning cold. They wanted away from the water's breeze.

At home, Carson went to put on her comfortable pajamas. It was movie night with her mom. She heard a knock on her window and knew it was Jody. She raised the window, and the night air instantly cooled her room.

"Have you been on Friender?"

"No, why? I'm just getting home."

"There's video of you today at school."

Carson booted up her computer. She stared at it with Jody, cringing as she watched the whole after-school confrontation.

"That's so embarrassing," Carson said.

"Read the comments." Jody slowly scrolled down the page.

Carson skimmed. It was an I-hate-Jessa campaign. All of her victims were coming forward. Some of them past friends. Some who had left Summit because of her. And others who had been afraid of becoming a target.

"Oh my! It worked. Emma and Mai said she'd come unglued. They told me that I would be the one to expose her."

"You planned this?" Jody asked proudly. "That's my girl. Never a victim!"

She didn't know if that was true. She had felt like a victim as she retreated to her bus. She had even felt like running away, but she hadn't. She read the comments again, proud of herself for outsmarting Jessa and taking away just a little of her power.

Carson knew that Jessa was somewhere out there reading the comments too. She had to realize that her reign of terror was coming to an end.

Chapter 13

The Hometown Favorite

Carson walked into Summit Middle School on Monday morning. Everyone seemed to know her name. She didn't know what to think.

"Hey, Carson!"

"What's up, Carson?"

Mai and Emma were waiting by their lockers with huge smiles on their faces. "It worked," Emma said proudly. "Everyone is on your side."

"Nobody wants to be Jessa's friend anymore. Even her own crew is turning against her," Mai added.

"She even has her own hashtag, the most beautiful bully."

Carson was a little less amused. It was just a matter of time before Jessa came up with another plan. She fully expected her to go down swinging. "I have a feeling this isn't over."

Later in the morning, Carson was pulled out of math. She had never been pulled out of class before. She was sure it wasn't good.

When she walked through the door of the front office, she saw her mom's face. She was now sure that she was in trouble. "Mom, what's wrong? What are you doing here?"

"I don't know. The school called me. Are you in trouble?"

"No," she said adamantly. Then she replayed the video in her head. She was afraid it would be used against her. The principal's secretary told them that she was ready to see them.

Mrs. Buckley said she was concerned about a video. It had been circulating over the weekend. Carson had played a big part in it.

Her mother's head turned quickly to her daughter. "You didn't mention a video."

Carson looked around nervously, not meeting her mom's eyes. Her mother knew that look. It meant trouble.

"Is there anything that you want to tell me before I press play?" Mrs. Buckley asked.

Carson shook her head, ready to let the chips fall where they may. Her mother watched the video in amazement as a group of girls surrounded her daughter. Her grip on Carson's hand tightened as the group closed in around her.

When it was over, she looked at her daughter through new eyes. She then turned her attention back to the principal.

"What are you going to do about this?" she asked Mrs. Buckley.

"I've already spoken with the young lady. She assures me that this will not happen again. She said that she was defending herself against Carson and her friends. Is that true, Carson?"

"She is a liar."

"She claims that you have been targeting her all week. I've made a lot of allowances for this program to work. I don't want my veteran students to feel threatened.

"Were we watching the same video? My daughter was the one targeted. And I didn't see any friends. I only saw one boy who was trying to protect her from that mob of girls."

Carson's face was buried in her hands. She felt like she was going to explode.

"Jessa is pure evil. She hates me. All of the girls here are afraid of her. She knows that she can get away with anything. She knows that you always will take her side." She looked directly at the principal. "Those are the allowances that are being made."

Carson showed the principal the Friender posts. She showed her what others had gone through because of Jessa. "That's who she is, Mrs. Buckley. You had to have known bullies when you were in school. She's a cheerleader. She's pretty. Her parents are rich. But she doesn't like herself. We are paying the price."

Her mom watched as Carson turned into a fighter right before her eyes. She proudly addressed the principal. "My daughter has said enough."

Mrs. Buckley stood up to let them out. She shook Mrs. Roberts's hand. "I didn't know."

"But you should have."

By the end of the day, they had all been called down, mean girl after mean girl. It was a parade. None of the girls reappeared in class. Jessa was the last one called into the principal's office. The rumors were true. Jessa's crew had turned on her.

"It was her idea!"

"I was just watching!"

"It was Jessa!"

They were all trying to save themselves from being labeled a bully. Jessa was the easiest to throw under the bus. Her actions had made it easy. They all pleaded down to a lesser sentence. They had been threatened with forty-five days at the alternative center. A three-day suspension seemed more doable.

Jessa and her mom retreated from the office, defeated and angry. "Your father will definitely have the last say on this one," she promised her daughter as they left the school with enrollment papers for her new school, Texsun Alternative Center (TAC).

Chapter 14

What Do You Want?

Carson and Holden sat under a huge oak tree during lunch. The holidays were approaching. Neither wanted to leave for the break without getting some idea about their relationship. He had questions. And she was finally ready to address them.

He played with a blade of grass as he gazed over the horizon, trying to avoid eye contact with Carson. He looked as if he had a lot on his mind. "You know there were a lot of rumors circulating after Jessa was sent to TAC."

"Yeah?" she asked, knowing that he wanted more.

"They say that you just used me to get to Jessa. That's what the guys are saying in gym."

"You've been so good to me, Holden."

He laughed. "You're not denying it. So it's true."

"No … I mean yes … I mean no." She began to shake her head.

"Well, which one is it? You either used me or you didn't."

"Listen, it started out that I was just hanging out with you to make her mad. We knew that you were her hot button."

"We? There were more people in on this? Y'all probably had a good laugh at my expense, huh? I believed that you liked me." He looked hurt, and she felt terrible.

"Holden, it wasn't like that. We were already friends. We were already hanging out, and then you offered to walk me to classes. It just kind of happened. I don't know."

"So, tell me the truth now. Jessa is gone. You don't have to hang out with me at all. What do you want?"

She thought about that for a while. Nobody had ever asked what she wanted before. Her mom and dad got a divorce. Nobody asked what she wanted. Her dad remarried and had a new baby. Still nobody asked what she wanted. The constables came to their house and kicked them out.

They bounced around from friend to friend. Lived off charity. Nobody asked Carson's opinion.

Then things started looking up. Her mother bought a smaller home in their old neighborhood. And this one was directly across the street from Jody. Recently, she replaced their broken-down car with a new convertible.

This question was definitely a first. What did she want?

"I want to hang out with you. I want to go places with you. I want you to meet Jody."

"Are you saying that you want me to be your boyfriend?"

"I don't know. I've never had a boyfriend before." He looked sad. "I don't even know what I'm supposed to do with a boyfriend. But you are the first guy I've ever wanted to get to know. You are the first person that I just can't seem to get enough of. Can we just start there and see where it takes us?"

He smiled. "We can do that. But hey, no more secrets."

"I promise. No more secrets." The bell rang. They walked back into the school with their fingers intertwined.

"Hey, Carson!" she heard as she walked through the halls.

"Hey!" she always replied happily, starting to fit in at her new school.

She descended the school's front stairs to meet up with Mai and Emma, ready for a sleepover at Emma's house. After three months at SMS, Carson had been through a lot. She had made some friends, gotten rid of an enemy, and learned a lot about herself along the way. She had to admit it, she liked Summit Middle School. She was still uncomfortable. She was still anxious. But she knew that she was going to be all right.

Want to Keep Reading?...

Turn the page for a sneak peek at Shannon Freeman's next book in the Summit Middle School series: *Silentious*.

ISBN: 978-1-68021-007-1

Chapter 1

A New Beginning

It was a cold, crisp day in Texsun City. Mai Pham sat in her room, listening to the crashing waves at the nearby beach. She was excited. More than excited. She was elated. She'd never felt this way before.

After Christmas break there was usually nothing to look forward to. Just the monotony of school. The kids at Summit Middle School were always so excited when they returned after the holidays. Mai thought about the delight in their voices as they caught up with friends and bragged about their gifts and vacations.

But Mai's life wasn't set up that way. Her family didn't even celebrate Christmas. Friends were minimal.

This year was different, though. In the fall a new student transferred to school: Carson Roberts. Mai knew she had found a kindred spirit. Quiet Emma Swanson felt the same way. Neither fit in with the popular cliques. But the three girls had created an unbreakable bond.

This semester Mai was happy to return to school. She was ready to see her new friends. They made her feel free, even though her parents, especially her father, kept her on a short leash.

Mr. Pham ran a tight ship. She dared not cross him. The first time she had ever disobeyed him was because of Carson. When the girls' PE lockers were broken into in the fall, her father ordered Mai to never hang out with Carson again.

But Mai went straight to her mother that very day, barging into her master suite. Her mom was in her enormous closet, choosing an outfit for a church meeting. You really couldn't call it a closet. It was more like another bedroom. It was that impressive. There were at least one hundred pairs of designer shoes, glass cabinets for her hand-bags, and a jewelry island in the center of it all. There was even a comfortable sitting area.

"Mom, Father is being unreasonable. You know I'm not to blame for my clothes being stolen. I did nothing wrong!" Mai had said.

"Calm down, Mai. I've already spoken with your father. Everything will be just fine," her mother had said. "I'll handle him."

"You didn't have my back at school. You never stood up for me."

"That wasn't the time. I needed the facts. I like Carson. Just don't let your father know that you two are still friends until I can win him over."

Mrs. Pham winked at her daughter. Mai threw herself at her mom and gave her a tight hug.

"Thank you, Mom!" she'd said excitedly.

To this day she had not received word that her new friendship was okay. So she kept her mouth shut. The last thing she wanted was for her father to find out. He was not to be disobeyed. But Carson and Emma were all she had. She wasn't going to give them up.

As Mai went downstairs for breakfast, she could hear her little sister talking. Lan was two years younger, but they looked a lot alike. With their heart-shaped faces, dark eyes, and silky black hair, they were striking.

The Pham girls clung to each other. There weren't any school events that they were allowed to attend: no socials, no carnivals, and no fundraisers. Their father was strict. If it wasn't an event with their church, they were not allowed to go. That meant many nights at home and many nights together.

The girls would fantasize about what life would be like if they were able to make their own decisions. They couldn't wait to turn eighteen. They both agreed they would go to the same college. They would always be there for each other, no matter what. High school graduation was many years away. So for now, they just had to deal with their father's rules.

Mai studied the massive school hallway as she headed to her locker. She searched for her friends but couldn't find them. She was disappointed. She was looking forward to the moment when they would reunite.

She was about to give up. Go to class.

Then she saw a mane of curly red hair coming her way. Emma. It couldn't be anyone else. Emma's face lit up when she spotted her friend. Carson was at Emma's side, waving like crazy. Mai smiled.

"There's Mai!" Emma yelled.

They were an unlikely trio. But maybe that's why they clicked. Mai, with her exotic features and long black hair. Carson, with her natural hair, twisting and turning into a regal African updo. And Emma, with a mass of dancing curls framing her face. They were very different. But they were drawn together by the knowledge that they were meant to be best friends.

Carson and Emma wore their feelings out in the open. First they hugged Mai. Then they blew air kisses. For Mai this was a first. Emotions were not meant for public display according to her father. His face was always unreadable. In public or private.

No way would Mai ever give up her girls. This was the first time a classmate had missed her. The first time anybody searched for her after a long break. And the first time she felt like she was actually a part of Summit Middle School. She needed it. Like air. She truly needed their love and friendship.

About the Author

Shannon Freeman

Born and raised in Port Arthur, Texas, Shannon Freeman is an English teacher in her hometown. As a full-time teacher, Freeman stays close to topics that are relevant to today's teenagers.

Entertaining others has always been a strong desire for the author. Living in

California for nearly a decade, Freeman enjoyed working in the entertainment industry, appearing on shows like *Worst-Case Scenario*, *The Oprah Winfrey Show*, and numerous others. She also worked in radio and traveled extensively as a product specialist for the Auto Show of North America. These life experiences, plus the friendships she made along the way, have inspired her to create realistic characters that jump off the page.

Today she enjoys a life filled with family. She and her husband, Derrick, have four beautiful children: Kaymon, Kingston, Addyson, and Brance. Their days are full of family-packed events. They also regularly volunteer in their community.

Freeman's debut series, *Port City High*, is geared to high-school readers. When asked to write for middle school students, she knew it would be a challenge, but one that she was up for. *Summit Middle School* is the author's second series. She hopes these stories will reach students from many different backgrounds. "It is definitely a series where middle-grade students can read about realistic life experiences involving characters just like them. Middle school can be a challenge, and if I can help students navigate through that world, then I have met my goal."

Freeman loves writing a series that her children and numerous nephews and nieces can enjoy.